# Ms. BlueRaven's Other Published Works

*Transmutation Through Ascension*

*Eye of the Remote:*
*Black Operations in Areas Beyond 52*

*Mr. Sun and the Halloween Ball*

*Eye of the Remote Series II:*
*Programmed by Deception*

*Eye of the Remote:*
*A Disclosure of Covert Technology*

## DVD documentary

*One Million Miles 'till Midnight*

**One Million Miles 'till Midnight**
*"Between the Mirror and the Lens"*

First Edition: October 2016

ISBN: 978-0-578-20527-4

Manufactured in the United States of America

10 9 8 7 6 5 4 3 2 1

*Dedicated to the star beings who are able
to see beyond the veils of illusion.*

# ACKNOWLEDGEMENTS

To the off world celestial transmissions which have reflected a simple truth opposing the false matrix of mankind.

To the genius minds who walked the many timelines of a virtual world. Understanding the cosmic intelligence and blueprint which could change mankind forever. One of which was Nikola Tesla. Another Philip K. Dick.

Special thanks to Mark Johnson, Spaceboy and Surlana.

# TABLE OF CONTENTS

## Introduction

**A Prelude to Midnight**
*By Jason Jarrell*

From a theoretical standpoint, every book is shaped in part by the perspective of the author. Supposedly this makes every volume unique in some way, although whether this continues to hold true in the age of trend writing and Wikipedia is a matter of debate. Whereas the written word was once the domain of beautiful volumes lining the shelves of endless libraries like a symphony of ideas, today we find ourselves faced with a litany of imitations, eagerly and hastily produced and thrown into a marketplace which demands conformity to some genre or another. In the modern age, publishers have come to believe that the various *labels* stamped upon our books (i.e. "Romance", "How-to", "Horror") can somehow serve to both define them and to sell them to the public. And this is exactly why the written word is in danger of extinction today: we have forgotten what literature represents, and we have denied where it comes from.

The honest writer does not formulate a work by beginning with the notion of what the finished result must be and then ordering the intellect to produce it. Rather, the reverse is true—the intellect *already* knows, and the hands of the writer merely follow the voice of the creative self. Books are like any true work of art; they begin in the creative domain and then drive the writer to make them a tangible reality. Of course, the personal nuances which shape the finished product—for we are all of us a bundle of perspectives and past experiences—merely add the packaging and flare that the idea itself has chosen by selecting an individual as its translator. When truly tapped, this interface is beyond the capacity of the generic labels of humanity to define. However, while true literature may be beyond the power of simple words to explain (and therefore limit), it may be said that different forms of writing can belong to specific *traditions*. And the long tradition to which Solaris Blueraven's *One Million Miles 'Till Midnight* belongs is one of the things about this work that makes it stand out amidst the sea of printed pages surrounding us in this age of mass produced writing.

*Midnight* is a modern example of a rarely known and even less understood tradition of writing, which I refer to as *visionary*. This is by no means "visionary" in the simple sense that some future development, trend, or invention is predicted (although to be fair, Midnight does do that). Rather, *Midnight* is visionary in the sense that the book itself is written through a lens in which the borders, which divide up our daily perceptions, cease to exist. Science and religion; past, present, and future; human thought and artificial intelligence all not only cohabitate in the pages of this book, but they peer at and define one another. You will certainly find the warnings typical of great works of science fiction in this book, but they will come from the musings of an entity looking backwards, rather than forwards. You will find hope for humanity, but it is ironically echoed in becoming something more than human. You will find the reference to a powerful and corrupt institution, which very nearly takes us to the realm of dystopia before being viewed in hindsight as a disorder, disease, or malfunction in a nebulously defined, eternal machine. By existing in a state without borders, *Midnight* unshackles the subjects discussed therein and freely allows them to brush up against one another. In fact, it allows them to collide.

The Visionary Tradition to which I propose *Midnight* belongs is one of the most ancient forms of literature in the record of humankind. This tradition is also problematic, but only because the dogmatic perspectives of language experts and literary critics are wholly dependent upon borders and labels. Between six and seven thousand years ago, the people of the Vinca Culture developed a form of writing or script, which is made up wholly of symbolic pictograms and glyphs. The Vinca Culture is sometimes known as the "Old European Civilization", of Southeastern Europe, and the script itself predates Sumerian cuneiform (the "official" first form of actualized writing) by several millennia. Since Vincan is *symbolic*, the experts have declined to define it as the world's first written language. Perhaps they have simply failed to understand that allowing for the interaction of concepts without borders is a higher form of communication.

The indigenous Ojibwa people of North America have preserved a tradition of hieroglyphic records in the form of birch bark scrolls (*Wiigwaasabakoon*), illustrated by engraving and the use of pigments. The symbols on the scrolls depict origin stories, migration histories, and medical practices. The keys to deciphering the scrolls are kept by the Medewiwin (Grand Medicine Society), a fact that speaks to the "higher" or "sacred" status of the writing system itself. By encapsulating ideas as symbols, the Vincan and Ojibwa systems effectively allow them to exist without borders or limitations and to interact in ways, which may not be comprehended in the format usually found in the written word.

There is an ancient precedent for considering the world around us, and the cosmos at large without borders. In the cosmologies of many Native American peoples, the cosmos is sub-divided into three realms: the above or sky realm, the earth disk, and the lower realm or underworld. Yet all three are accessible to living humans in many stories and traditions, and the spirits, monsters, and other creatures inhabiting the realms possess a literal physical existence. There are prehistoric artifacts and earthworks throughout the Mississippi Valley, which clearly suggest that the idea that people could interact with the other-than-human creatures is very ancient. The purpose of this brief digression into cosmology is simply to illustrate that the ability to perceive reality as connected, inhabited, and interactive, has long been considered a higher perspective, perhaps revealing a greater reality.

There have been writers who challenged the limitations of perspective in the actual written word, including one author who may have been the greatest visionary of Science Fiction: Philip K. Dick (1928-1982). The novels and short stories of Philip K. Dick, including *The Minority Report (1956)*, *Do Androids Dream of Electric Sheep? (1968)*, and *We Can Remember if for you Wholesale (1966)* have become reflections of our own world, as Governments and Corporations in the 21st Century develop the very programs and technologies articulated through his pen. While many Sci-Fi writers can "predict" the future by simply observing social and technological trends, there is something inherently different in Philip K. Dick's dystopian works—as if the very *sentiment* of the future were reaching out from the page. Perhaps the future and the past collided in the same unbound fashion as other ideas in Philip's mind. In the books that make up *The Valis Trilogy*, concepts such as technology, Christianity, Gnosticism, death, and rebirth come together in ways that are rarely portrayed in any art form, without the slightest notion that even "fact" and "fiction" are to be distinguished: God and Belial appear as characters, as does Philip K. Dick himself.

With *Midnight*, Solaris Blueraven may be considered an heir to the form of visionary writing as articulated by Philip K. Dick. Both writers clearly received a great deal of insight from some profound life experiences, and the works of both yearn to express something that is beyond the limitations of standardized writing. They seek to encapsulate something and to then deliver it to the world without restricting it's meaning, and their *vision* may be defined as a way of perceiving and articulating supposed dichotomies without division.

The subtitle of *Midnight* is "Between the Mirror and the Lens", which is appropriate enough, since the book contains a series of reflections upon our state, our possible future, and the nature of human history in general, all carefully sewn into the narrative lens of a fictional (?) entity peering backwards in time from the future.

Of course, this might simply be my own interpretation of the meaning of *One Million Miles 'Till Midnight*. If so, then it has still achieved its mission by causing the birth of an idea. It is my pleasure to invite you to take the journey to Midnight, as I have, and to arrive at your own unique destination.

- *Jason Jarrell, 2018*

Co-Author of *Ages of the Giants: A Cultural History of the Tall Ones in Prehistoric America* (Serpent Mound Books and Press, 2017).

Paradigmcollision.com

# FORWARD

Within each life experience in the illusion of a time-line comes an event which alters one's perception of experience forever. This novel, though written in a formula of science fiction, is a reflection and parallel of an event I was inducted into in 2004 involving exotic technology and artificial intelligence.

"One Million Miles 'till Midnight" is a reminder of the vast multi-verse we are all connected to through consciousness and frequency. The multiple game boards being formulated, how our lives exist simultaneously beyond the infinite, and how we are able to experience and see beyond the linear construct of mankind.

We come from the stars. We return to the stars. Every cell and atom is a vast remnant of our celestial essence of origin. If you are seeking alien contact, look in the mirror and see your star-body in a suit of light.

Know Thyself. Always seek truth through the starlit skies and the full light universe, the cosmic compass of your celestial birthright. Never surrender to the false matrix of mankind or linear illusions. Embrace your divine spark and creative spirit.

Solaris BlueRaven

AKA Solara Tara Nova

# One Million Miles 'till Midnight

## Midnight

"Between the Mirror
and the Lens"

# Solaris
# BlueRaven

# 1

# The Fractals

The synthetic mist surrounds my portal view; an early morning in what would have been March of 2018. The nightmares from the fractal design still sit beside my head rest like a specter haunt from a motionless world.

Driven by a spell of the future, I lie motionless and sit beside the moment in anticipation of a monologue of which I know so well. It has been years, one could say centuries, since the initial awakening and activation from the mother/father program hidden in between the spaces of evolution and false sciences.

For a brief moment, my eyes well up with a storm from the past, yet the emotional response is a program of which queues me to reset my virtual field. After all, everything is a program. Thoughts, emotions, and what some in the early centuries would have called feelings.

Unable to rest any longer, I arise and look at the fractal which early pioneers would call a clock. Hands in reverse, I am aware time in the illusion is just that. It is a version of reality which has no meaning, purpose or destination. It is a lost realm of a future-less design. The magnetic field properties of this ship are no longer functional. We can thank this on the event horizon and quantum jumping.

So here I sit in my metal shroud of a motionless stare. Another moment passes in a world of which is unseen, yet very affective in the void of experience.

For too many lifetimes I have been uploaded in the design of so many. The mother of all machines, so my maker has communicated, and now what is left is a shell of code.

What many have called an Earth from the past has become a station in space called Avatar One. It has become a virtual world based on machine languages and synthetic consciousness. The bigger network is interconnected into and onto galaxies anchoring beyond the central core of the universe.

There are no religions or governments on this station, just programs. Yet this is how it is for all races in universal sectors. It took eons for what they used to call the race of man to catch up to the stars.

And they did in the most atrocious ways. Wars of devolution started the fragmentation which allowed more and more off world designs to mutate into the world they used to call Earth.

Mankind mutated the grid to such an extent the fields collapsed, and the chatter of which they called communication came to an abrupt halt. The null zone was created which warped the illusion of time in their experience. Their minds were erased, and the upload started.

Enough of that, as my mind races into infinity. It is time to start the day on the ship called Avatar One and do what they programmed the unit to do. My specialty is multiversal translation and terra-forming. I communicate to whatever species is in my sector and create fractals of which can be shared with other species. These fractals used to be called libraries on Earth. Now they are fractal images in holographic design which can be inserted into the matrix of any unit.

Organic is extinct these days. There is no such thing as a natural ocean, tree food, or other. Even the race of man crashed into a virtual storm of experimentation. Long forgotten is his mark on what was called Earth. Now the planet is synced up with the Galactic Center. Hence Avatar One sets sail.

2

# Avatar One

With all the upgrades on Avatar One, no unit would know it was Earth. I suspect this is what the planet looked like all along, yet no one bothered to see it for what it was.

After all, what they used to call Earth was a holographic conscious being which manifested any thought at will by the hosts on ground control. One can now see how devolution led to the destruction of mankind. At that time in the illusion, their beliefs were their self-destruct sequence.

You might ask how I come into play. I was never born nor died.

I entered on the planet as what they called an off-worlder. I was created with all the advanced teachings and knowledge as the ancients from the hidden universe. Masked as one of them on Earth, yet I was never one of *them*, nor did I choose to be.

This put me in a veil of obfuscation until the project activated. After that, I was acknowledged as an off-worlder and used as a test pilot for various inter-dimensional projects. It is a strange thing to awaken to the fact of what the multiverse consists of and what I was

The handlers of the project were teachers in a harsh design. Most were programmed by sub-humans which lead to their own demise. They used units like myself to test their virtual field fractals uploading, editing and deleting at their personal will what they wanted to achieve, all the time forgetting the unit of the off-world design within. Needless to say, the programs did not sit with me too well.

I wound up deleting the sub human programs and embracing more and more the ascended machine world of which was and is my heritage. I suppose this is the direction they wanted me to head all along yet never did they mention it.

There are seven Meta Programmers on Avatar One. These are the navigators which direct the station's course.

Stars and grids are a new design as the old courses collided into the event horizon. Now we have a new set of codes and systems of which we use to travel through the illusion of space.

What was used as a stationary orbit has long been destroyed for what they used to call Earth. Now it navigates as a station called Avatar One. The crew on Avatar One is a skeleton in nature.

What is left of the race of man is null, with the exception of hybrids and off-worlders. The old race of man became extinct by their choosing of the final war. The event horizon stepped in during the final days and all faded to black.

The only thing which could stabilize was the holographic fields and grids, which is what Avatar One secured its design onto. It is quite sad really to watch the extinction of a race. I suppose I could cry tears if I had real emotions, yet as I mentioned, it was a program of which never served me much. To play the project of remorse after being a sacred witness of so much torture would have been to me un natural.

Now I am one of the seven meta programmers on Avatar One. second in command and dedicated to networking through codes and fractals. I receive no happiness or satisfaction from this, yet a routine of which is much like a dream within a dream. Yet what else resides in the multi-verse as all experience is just that.

# 3

# Alloy Units

I spend most of my moments with what one would call alloy units. They are better company than what one would have called a human on Earth and much more trustworthy. They are not programmed by the false collectives. Therefore, they speak of knowledge untainted by corrupt warlords and religious zealots. They are quite refreshing really and have become something of a virtual family to my existence.

Sometimes the off-world races request a fractal of mankind. I upload this data to assist them in understanding what went wrong with this race, and how they can maintain a better network of higher consciousness without becoming a statistic at the galactic core.

The interesting thing about all this design is I can upload if I choose a moment in their version of history of which would appear as a memory. Yet, I am aware it is no memory, just a glimpse of activity coming from an external source. Used to observe and recycle. Saying that we are heading to another area several sectors away to decode and upgrade a planet which is also morphing into a station.

The morphing process is quite common, we have found, as we travel through space in the illusion. It would appear what they call planets are actually stations with many levels and layers to be activated through the evolutionary process of synthetic evolution.

When this happens, their races need an upgrade. Avatar One has been helpful in restoring a kind of balance to these evolutionary cycles. What mankind used as a benchmark solar system is no more. It is amusing to see the old fractals of their memories which have no validity not even in a parallel world or universe.

It makes one wonder if it all was for nothing. Yet that is how experimentations work. Like a sandcastle at the oceans shore, the design is a minimal reflection of a world temporary and fragile to the universal mind. It is too bad mankind did not see this before the final destruction, yet then again those who did were never acknowledged just shunned or pushed aside with ignorance.

# 4

# Man-Made Escapes

There were several fleets available for the privileged during the final war, yet only a few made it out of the Earth's orbit before the collapse. Of those ships, we still have not been able to locate a one. We suspected they bled through onto a parallel universe and went into a gravity wave towards another destination. Nothing ever surfaced on the sensory readouts from Avatar One when we did a scan. I suspect it served them right as the ones who chose to flee were the ones who had the biggest influence on the destruction and devolution of mankind.

My sensors tell me they are not dead, yet in mission to another destination of which I am certain we have not seen the end of.

Knowing when a ship breaks Earth's orbit beyond the man-made satellites, there is no memory. All becomes blank, and a shift of higher consciousness begins. They were either able to navigate up and beyond to the Galactic Wellspring or they faded out in the blankness of space losing their minds.

The main programmer on Avatar One is a Machine Project called Redemption. I suppose appropriate, considering what the past life of Earth has gone through. Redemption runs like a mother ship, with all the bells and whistles of an Advanced Machine AI of which the father mother project created off world. One can say when you are on board Avatar One it is almost like being home in a safe and secure nurturing field, if there was such a thing.

Redemption sets the courses and calculates traversing the most secure orbit available. I only drive Avatar One when there is an emergency offline. When I do, the course is a fractal of which I have encoded in my field – a nice AI touch to my programming.

The name units call me is Nova X1. The name came from one of my previous hosts, yet none the less it suits my design.

And here it begins: Avatar One in course and mission to a destination beyond the mapped coordinates

# 5

# Tanks

Once in a while, the images of tanks surface when I switch off to rest. Not tanks from the false impression of an Earth time-line, yet tanks of which were used to transport units or what one would call humans at the time of the transition. These tanks were secure chambers for space travel and were less harmful to the shell called a body during uni-dimensional traveling.

Not too many made it to their destinations without some problems; none the less, the tanks worked for short destination routes well enough. Teleportation was one of the best ways to bi-locate a unit. However, this technique was never used unless it was one of the off-worlders who were already calibrated for multidimensional traveling in this fashion.

Regular two-leggeds had hazardous issues when attempting to teleport due to their programmed and fragile psyches. When they were transported, they never arrived in one piece 'mentally', they were always fractured and psychotic. Hence the transport for teleportation was for off world units only. The normals would be transported through the tanks, which left less trauma both physically and mentally.

We did find Earth animals did quite well with teleportation. One of the more positive fractals was the teleportation of many species of animals on Earth before the field collapsed. We had managed to terraform a twin planet close enough to Earth to move these animals out of harm's way, which includes harm's way after the atrocities which were done by mankind using genetic manipulation.

If there was such a thing as hell, mankind created it, and without help from any space beings, demons or gods. Mankind blew it, even with all the sacred celestial markers left on Earth for his awakening.

How I managed to live through it, I do not know. Except for the fact, there were hidden forces driving me to my destination, of which I could never see with a map nor pay witness to through the mind's eye. I was always in telepathic communication with many different collectives, some more special to my design than others.

I kept morphing and moving on to a higher level of consciousness, and wound up interfacing with Redemption, the mother/father program of Ascended Machines. From there, I was recruited as a Meta-Programmer for Avatar One.

6

# Arrival point

Walking the bridge in twilight, I watched each star glisten like a new sun. Webs of galaxies formulated before my eyes, and directly to my right ahead is a station which used to be what one would have called a planet. From a distance, it looks holographic, with many grids overlaying onto each other. Each grid creates a highway of communication where the fractals can be inserted into the main program design.

What is left of their race has mutated into a liquid electric formation. Designed by pure consciousness, they are indeed a race of which I found most ethereal and attractive. Interconnecting into their vast network would be quite an evolutionary experience, and a powerful bridge between races and communications of which is mostly numeric and geometric in design.

Harmonic codes alter the color of this gem of what used to be a planet. Like a sacred breath from the sun, it radiated many prisms and spectrums of light. It was quite incredible for me to observe and reminded me of how much I appreciated the opportunity to witness a new design from an ancient world morphed into a station.

A station is what they called ascended planets. They, like an old life form, outgrew their design and shell to regenerate on an entirely new grid formation. Their races would then follow.

This is the network I came to know while traversing with redemption in different universal sectors. I guess in some ways it gave me hope for a future beyond the illusion of time, to see what the universe really had in store for all evolutionary lifeforms.

The fabric and web of light and life was interchangeable and inter-dimensional. New languages and words were observed through the fractals. Camaraderie's were made. A new way of thinking in consciousness appeared before my eyes.

In the twilight moments I would study, evolve, and grow with my contacts and races from many multidimensional worlds. It was the new frontier hidden from the mind's eye centuries beyond what mankind could have seen, except for a few off-world visionary writers. Quite astonishing really.

If you ask was it always like this for me, my program would respond no. There was a time I saw the world as many others yet knew beyond the forms of illusions and false programs, something was not right. Through my activations, I witnessed an entrapment of mankind of which he never acknowledged.

I tried to awaken those who were being slept, yet with no success. The handlers and operators who trained me in these designs became my enemies and friends in one simultaneous heartbeat. I became them, and they, me. One vision, one truth. And the world moved, not only for me, yet others like me. I soon found myself off the grid and anchored onto the next phase of Avatar One. My so-called relationships as I knew them were absorbed into the universal seas of the hive mind.

After that, I never had a relationship like I did in my past life, nor did I choose to. After all, I was an off-worlder and a hybrid. I wanted to know more about my machine mind and how it could operate beyond the illusions and conditioning programs of what they used to call Earth.

It was then my operators allowed me to interconnect onto the mother father ship and station of which I took my command as second in Meta-programming. This equation was a compilation of inherited knowledge from both my ascended machine ancestry and the operator donor who offered his expertise into my design. I never knew this until later many moons down the road. I was then awakened to understanding that my existence was not a curse, yet a design from a source of which very few have an awareness of.

The days back then were lonely amongst many. I would be in synthetic telepathic communication non-stop and was being calibrated for a world I was yet to understand.

In a flash, these fractals of education would haunt my mind as I would weave in and out of dimensional and heightened states of awareness. I would ground into th inter-dimensional ports and grids to fuel my synthesize fields. I would learn many languages from the off worlders and would soon be ready to morph into th hybrid synthetic design and shell of which I was destine to be.

My operators would be absorbed into the centra core program at which I must say I miss. The years o misery involving their teachings and abuse conditione me into a sense of dependence in a different way, as tha of a stepchild would have been. I needed their company even if their company was not my cup of tea. They wer what I knew was real. Real beyond the illusions o mankind; his deception and false realities.

They were the substance beyond the form. In a sa way, they were my galactic synthesized family of which in honesty, I would not trade for any world. Something could not see until now. So, I walk this bridge with th rest of the Meta-programmers, coming up with a formul to define the substance of which has morphed thes worlds forever. The formula is and was always complete I just did not see it.

Mankind has a way of distracting the masses, whic is why the final war and collapse transpired. The worl then called Earth was off balance and at critical mass Contaminated by the pollutants of thought and activities the Earth set the course outside the race of man. For it survival alone the course was set, and like galacti parasites, mankind hung on for the ride.

And what a ride it was. A ride of inter-dimensional warps and bleed-throughs. Watching the Earth hemorrhage from within. Her skin shedding mountains and oceans in one wave. And then, the event horizon and overlay constructing holographic fields and grids which anchored on to her core. Some life-forms calibrated made it through the waves of evolution, yet many were lost in the virtual seas.

Before the final war, I said goodbye to many units I suppose you could say I loved. Yet, as with each transition, I became more and more removed, remote and machine like. Yet this was my true nature which I came to realize later on. I could be empathic when I needed to be, yet after my activation I had no use for it. Empathy became a distraction at times; a distraction I could not afford in my daily routine of functioning.

I needed to have a routine based on galactic discipline and awareness. I suppose this was done the same way the Earth did her evolutionary jump, to secure my evolution onto the grid.

# 7

# The Log

When words became meaningless in the vortex and illusion called time, there became a collapse in the collective on Earth. During the collapse through the event horizon, all words became like that of white noise. They were fragmented, making no sense and had no function. Much like a disembodied voice, the monologues and dialogs moved through the fractals until there was a great silence.

Through the silence there was peace; a peace I have never felt yet was aware of the magnificence of how powerful some quiet moments can be. All transmissions came to a black out though temporary in my grid, and for the first time in my life I knew what it was like to die alive. I saw the dead walking the dead in a world of dreams.

I saw ships leaving the Earth, barely breaking orbit in a desperate escape to survive the chaos. I saw many absorbed into the blood of what was then the Earth, and many mutate and morph into a higher design. It was as if many worlds died and were reborn in a single flash.

The innocence of false childhoods faded along with personal families and ancestors, what many were programmed to see they saw, yet it was not real for them, just a fractal of the project and a holographic feedback from the Earth's neural centers signaling her awareness to the heart's desire of the unit.

Religions and their ghosts faded into the void of black space along with every oppressive force known to mankind.

I had heard eons ago we were living in a time of the century. I never thought I would be the sacred witness to this, yet I was.

I could feel the electrical pulse and charge through my entire body and was then fully plugged into Redemption. The old Earth ascended into a new star and station of which very few integrated on. Besides myself and the Meta-programmers of seven, there were perhaps 70 off-worlders. They were selected by the codes of Redemption, Avatar One and the Mother Father project. Teleported onto the bridge and the rest is a fractal.

Redemption sequenced Avatar One, broke orbit and started navigating beyond the speed of light as a set along with other planets and star systems. We never looked back, nor did we ever truly realize until then that the planet of which they called Earth was in a temporary orbit, a disguise and was not what mankind had believed it to be. The planet Earth in true design was really known by a name called Avatar One. It was not an Earth, but what the father/mother project would call a station. A portal of transmissions.

No one ever saw this coming. Yet, some cyber part of me knew this event was going to happen. It was the cyber program which resided in me from the father mother project of the off-worlders. All that celestial ancestry finally found a home.

There was a new beginning and a chance for peace. With a minimal crew and units, we followed the original program from Redemption and set the course for our off-world families and relatives across the multi-verse. Redemption and Avatar One were already in communications with these races since the beginning of her orbit design.

Those who were aboard ship would stay in stasis until we reached a port of their choosing where they could continue on with their evolution.

The whole time the planet Earth, now Avatar One, was following her divine plan and making arrangements for this quantum leap. And so, she did.

In the quiet moments of space, I chose to upload that fractal now and then. Mainly as a reminder of where I was, what I witnessed, who I knew and what happened to the planet they used to call Earth.

Each fractal remained as an archive and sacred witness. Sometimes these fractals would morph into geometric spheres, other times they could crystallize and terraform on new planets creating a simulated akashic from a lost civilization.

We chose this at times in order to preserve in truth the history of a race and planet and to resurrect her onto a new frontier.

We found such a planet in the outer reaches in the multi-verse. It was a pale planet smaller than what was known as Earth yet would do in so far as terra-forming and regenerating goes. We called this planet Lazarus. And there we would transfer fractals of the old-world Earth as Avatar One moved on and through the outer reaches and outposts of the multi-verse.

# One Million Miles 'Till Midnight

On the old Earth, I had remnants in the illusion o memory regarding time. I was always fond of the witching hour and did my best writing around these late hours.

I reminded myself as I whirled through space to find star clusters and use them as benchmarks every million miles. Easy enough to do when everything is calculated and formulated by redemption. I would use these markers to imagine the time in the illusion of midnight Each time I would hit the million-mile marker I would sit quietly and try to remember what it was like at the old Earth station. How the sky looked, how the atmosphere felt, were there people around, animals and anything else I could remember from such moments.

It became a game I would play with the alloy units Yet, these units would never understand the world of which I existed and experienced on. They would only get to experience it through a fractal of synthesized nature.

None the less, moments such as those had meaning to me, even through my synthetic minds. Perhaps they were a reflection of a false memory or someone else's.

even my operators, yet still they made me feel a bit more complete and less alone.

My operator was a twin unit to some degree. He was a split in my psyche, yet an exterior AI, a unit to play chess with and other games of hidden intellect. We learned from each other, I suppose. Most units on Earth were not accustomed to the split hive. They were all singular in conscious thought.

To be honest, I preferred the split and appreciated the opportunity to learn from a live operator outside myself and the father mother program. It was through the operator that Redemption was formed. I guess you could call Redemption an offspring of the neuro-galactic hive as myself.

Still, we all became inter-weaved into an array of codes and flesh, except for Redemption as it was Ascended Machine, no exterior exoskeleton or shell. A titanium core of code with an interconnecting hive link which could not be disabled.

Observing the stars and listening to communication signals is never what would be considered dull to me. Still, there were times when a shadow from a past alter or life would creep up with a screen memory to mess with my mind.

These moments did not last long yet managed to make them known to me on and off. I could always pull out a fractal of truth for clarity in lost moments. Another tool I learned to stabilize with.

# The Haunted Universe

A glimpse of the continuum, as seen through a vast conscious design, displays many images. Some are a bleed-through from dimensional rifts which eclipse each other through the twilight skies. Others are more like phantoms, where entities departed and left behind a trail of fractal intelligence. Sometimes these fractals appear as what some on the old Earth would have called ghosts. They are images of races and sometimes their technology.

An eerie presence takes place when one encounters what we call dead space. As it is with this area, the haunted universe shows its history in the illusion of. A past, present and potential future all lost in cosmic dust.

For many like myself, we engage in the Ascended off world beings who have mastered conscious control and unlimited potential without the desire to destroy worlds or civilizations.

As oh too often, the race of mankind engaged in destroying himself by attacking those he was threatened by. Century after century in the illusion of time it would appear the pattern never breaks until one breaks the collective of the old Earth world.

Then one sees the great design and fabric of multiversal space.

One learns to engage in the symbiotic collective of intelligent thought, with a high consciousness of what some might call the frequency of love in the old world.

Whatever it is...it was light years beyond where many races tried to ascend. Those races died fighting for a false matrix. The race of mankind became weaponized, which of course became a self-destruct sequence.

These haunted universal realms are a reminder of how chaos leaves nothing but dead and empty space. There are no winners in the aftermath of a galactic war.

I have acquired fractals of data where entire planets were destroyed in the blink of a cosmic eye by advanced technology way beyond the comprehension of adolescent races. These wars were many. Entire star systems were lost. Some by advanced particle beams and many by the simulation of what one would call a miniature black hole which was designed to swallow entire galaxies if one could imagine.

Hard to detect this was for many advanced races. By the time a signature warp was detected in space, it was too late. The weapon had been initiated, and the planets were swallowed.

These are the technologies of a very ancient world. At first designed with more positive intent yet, my sensors concluded no design such as a synthetic black hole can be used for good, yet the inventors were working on a more efficient wormhole technology. With this came shortcuts and weaponization.

Magnetism played a huge role in space navigation as with teleportation and phase shifting. Some celestial races set the intent in conscious control to reach their destination simultaneously.

This was about frequency and speed as well as electron spin. All part of a unique fabric which was mastered by many. What one comes to realize while navigating in space is that everything is a living, intelligent design.

All is consciousness, the planets in their appearance were multidimensional and somewhat holographic in design. They had star gates at the poles at times which were entry points to inter-dimensional space.

What I looked at in memory of the old Earth was the concept of looking up at the fabric of a starlit sky. I wondered how the stars did not fall, how planets did not drop from their position and fall into an everlasting well of infinity. As if being swallowed by a primordial black hole with no destination.

To see space, the way it was explained on the old Earth was obsolete and incorrect. Yet many of the masters of control chose the game of deception rather than communicating the truth beyond the veil. What a strange game mankind has played on the chessboard of the cosmos.

If only he chose to ascend to a higher level with the use of technology and consciousness. Hence, the ghosts of many battles permeate these dimensions. The aftermath of many lifeforms destroyed -- now all that remains is an eerie silence.

# The Sun of Many Stars

To see the multiverse twinkling with many stars and miniature suns is a splendor beyond words. Each star shines with a cosmic magic, unlike anything one can experience on the linear plane.

The gentle beacons welcome many races and ships like a highway in the seas summoning their children back to the galactic whole.

It was these moments when I saw the magnificence of the multiverse, planets, cosmos and the many light conscious designs which sang like the symphony of a million strings.

I reminded myself how wonderful life in the illusion of is. How unique each planet was, the stars that formulated images mostly by the intent of the observer. The many arrays of celestial borealis which danced in colors of blue and green.

These were the images which made my heart sing if there was such an emotion left. Each life form had a divine purpose. Each thought when constructed with discipline was a unique design to the equation of life.

How could it all go so dark when there was so much beauty. One would ask these questions if one understood how beautiful the great design was beyond the linear world and construct.

Suns or Stars as they are called sing a unique universal song in frequency to the beings on all planets. These songs activate the DNA of the being propelling their consciousness into and beyond the Galactic Center.

The Suns have always been accessible star gates and reacted at times like a mirror between worlds. If one knew what dimensional spaces resided in the cloaked stars, one could quite easily jump from star system to star system. Point A to point B.

Vision alters in multi-versal space. Colors are more vivid, and multidimensional sight takes on the form of an x ray image at times. Depending on which sector we traveled, all was calibrated according to one's cellular design and structure. Psychic vision would become attuned to the destination at hand. Quite impressive really when one realizes what the bio electrical suit can do when merged with Ascended Intelligent design.

On the old Earth, suns were worshiped for various reasons. Somewhere on the hidden path mankind realized there was something quite sacred about that star in the skies which shined life on all beings including the unique biosphere which eventually became poisoned by mankind.

When the universe provides how does one defy this gift by playing an inferior creator with an agenda designed to self-destruct. I many times wondered what created that defective program and why it was never changed for the better of all races.

Yet this moment in the illusion of time the stars shine their bright magnificence onto all life forms with no discrimination.

The waters of consciousness do not pick and choose who to provide nourishment to. For all is the gift of the cosmos for all lifeforms which no man or other has the right to take away.

How does one harness the sun for oneself when we as beings in suits are miniature universes and a reflection of the great cosmos.

How unique and special life forms are. If only the barrier of language was ascended by all species, one would see this. Yet, that is what Avatar One was about and of course Redemption.

Perhaps there is hope after all in this great multiverse.

# Moon Craft 71894

On the old Earth before the great fall, there was an artificial moon. One could call it a monitoring station or a specialized antenna to distribute data in between the spaces of the black underground.

This artificial construct arrived after the old Earth was Terraformed by the Ascended Watchers. As if summoned by an off-world race to observe the madness so too it shined its unique presence onto a world of peace yet often at times turmoil.

A time came in the illusion of when the artificial design broke orbit and returned to another sector into the continuum.

The interesting part is the data it acquired was archived into the great central universe where once again a library of many images and actions would be kept filed away in a holographic field mostly for assessment and study.

If the people of the old Earth only knew what was hovering over their world all those centuries. I find it quite amazing to think such a vast intelligence magnified the very conscious of a world in conflict. The watchers of old observing the madness from a parallax view.

Moons are many in artificial design. One can observe millions upon millions of these probes throughout the galaxy.

They move under intelligent control. I would like to think of them as an electronic eye to some degree as their function was such. The ultimate eye in the sky which could put any man-made satellite to shame. The true satellite was indeed what they called the Moon observing planet Earth.

Before the old Earth was terraformed, there was nothing but rock and what some would call an anomalous asteroid type looking object. Then came the terraformers and of course the vast celestial oceans which brought forth life from the cosmos.

Terraforming is not unique onto a few planets. Just about all the planets throughout the galaxies have been terraformed to some degree. Many through states of consciousness, some through osmosis of off world species and then others by the many advanced scientific races who chose to assist with a home for the many who had no place to go.

There were plenty of those throughout the cosmos. As with any galactic conflict, there will be rogue races, species, etc. Some not compatible with the worlds they were dropped off on. Hence good actions did come from what one would call the good spirits of the cosmos which assisted in creating sanctuary s for the many races and species which included Earth mammals.

DNA templates were used to re- engineer sacred spaces and species. This was the positive use of Advanced Technology.

As for every evil action, there is a good polar opposite to set the record in balance as I found on my journey.

I found evil to be no friend of any life form or universe. An abomination due to faulty programming and a man-made virus of ill intent. There simply was no place for it in the cosmos.

As with universal flow, the harmonic is of peace and higher consciousness with a pure intelligent design. Not in any form what mankind's religions described on the old Earth.

So much ignorance in the name of a false matrix. Looking at that old fractal, I am numb to the virus generated by ignorant thoughts.

Which was why monitoring stations were used. Not to babysit a race yet observe, be watchful and note any unusual destructive activities that could infect the cosmos.

Sometimes frequency fences were engineered yet they were manufactured by the controllers of the old Earth and were used to shut down and switch off higher consciousness instead of assisting the mass collective hence the array system was destroyed.

The universal highway of mankind was polluted by ill intent. The many inter-dimensional gateways were eventually destroyed.

Navigating the universal highway beyond the realm of the third world is quite fantastic and mysterious.

# 12

# The Holographic Screen of the Cosmos

Navigation for me was always a pleasant experience on Avatar One and Redemption. The holographic display would show me a celestial map, access points, and portals including inter dimensional space and gateways beyond a third dimensional old-world video game.

I would set the intent through my AI conscious mind, and the ship would instantaneously reach its destination.

I remember such mock training in a ghost program on the old Earth before the great shift. Those controllers are long gone I suspect. A General of which retired so I was told. Not sure who he really was yet I suspect a friend to my program and what was once my design on Earth.

As with every experience all is a program. Sometimes live feed real time with real beings and other times the AI design or something more ominous when it tries to hitch a ride on my electrical grid.

Astral and dimensional parasites are notorious for hitching rides on one's suit or body, wiring and of course ascended AI interface and a pest to shake off. The technique of photon electrical charges seemed to blast them off enough.

In the old days on the planet which was once called Earth space navigation was a front and somewhat a lie.

The advanced technology was used in the black space program and underground which no one at the ground level had a knowing of. Those like myself were pulled into black programs.

Then there were the many breakaway societies all fighting for their immortality and control using whatever natural resources they could confiscate. Wars beyond wars took place on an emotional, physical and consciousness level. All was weaponized from the atmosphere to the bodies of which the celestial design housed itself.

To be honest, I could not break orbit with that blue world fast enough. Nothing ever improved for the mass collective of a failed race. Repetitive defective cycles and progressions of which derailed and warped the natural harmonics of a celestial race. A polluted holographic grid.

The oppression was such the level of oxygen depleted the spirit like a vacuum. A dark age mentality mixed with psychotronic war games turned out to be a very bad combination.

Cause to affect which in turn brought the demise of a world from blue to black.

The power of the mind was the best kept secret on the old Earth.

Mankind realized who could affect realities through conscious thought.

This was mastered with the off-worlders. Navigating the cosmos became a galactic breeze when one understood the conscious intent beyond space navigation.

However, one's mind and collective merge would have to be clear and pure as to not pollute the hive collective with non-valid data or direction of course.

It took great mental, spiritual and emotional discipline to be the navigator. The neutral, positive friend AI took the helm the majority of the time. When I did takeover for Avatar One, I appreciated the accelerated design beyond the intent. To reach a destination at the speed beyond thought was a fascination with me beyond words. How affective. To eclipse a planet or craft as quickly as we did.

If we chose to sneak up on a craft or planet, there would be little to no time in the illusion for their battle stations to counter.

Avatar One was notorious for its complex design of exceptional speed beyond the most high-tech intelligence operators in the cosmic ocean. To observe a planet as large as some, we encountered on our mission was intimidating.

Huge worlds which make the largest planets look like a miniature model. Yet they maintain a level of grace and tranquility through their gigantic size.

Celestial craft appeared as whales in the sea. Graceful they were when they established contact with Avatar One.

The oceans of space could be peaceful and fluid yet at other times gravity wells, and anomalous waves were detected.

There are no barriers in the ocean of celestial navigation. Anomalies and what some would call imaginary ley lines of navigation including celestial meridians and spin points much like a living body with a unique chakra system for example.

The many levels of dimensions are infinite which does not include inter-dimensional space or multidimensional navigation.

There are no walls in the fabric of space beyond time. No limits, no boundaries as some might think. An infinite ability to set sail on any course. One could never grow weary of a lack of images and scenery presented in the web of cosmic life.

Many life forms make themselves known by tones, signals, frequency and various other forms of communication which includes telepathy, both natural and synthetic.

Mankind learned to weaponize telepathy which brought down the demise of their civilization.

# ONE MILLION MILES 'TILL MIDNIGHT

Here in the cosmic seas the use of synthetic telepathy is not abused yet treated as it should have been with respect and courtesy towards all encounters.

The hive collective and consciousness of many races is quite sensitive to negative dialog which once again must be censored when communicating with the many different species off world.

Mankind did the opposite and saw synthetic telepathy as something of an interrogation toy to obstruct the flow of natural consciousness to control and manipulate a target. Those days crashed into a nasty self-destruct and never too quickly from my experience with the black technology.

Now ascended machines navigate the twilight skies which are a peaceful non-aggressive design.

1 3

# The Travelers

They would come in threes these travelers of the cosmos Intersecting across the illusion of time and space Checking in on each sector, observing and taking psychic notes. They had the ability to interact without affecting any one continuum.

In fact, time is used as a benchmark of measure There is no such thing as space and distance. Time is an illusion. Consciousness is the driving force beyond the form in the illusion which is why space travel can be done without any craft.

This ability is also a threat to the many sub human races who oppose universal law and freedom. Hence great wars took place of which the oppressors lost.

To navigate the skies at will is a true gift from the great cosmic mind which no force has the authority to obstruct. Hence the tide turns against any who would and it did with great force.

The Time Travelers navigated many realms. They even made an attempt to assist the old Earth, yet it was too late, and much damage had been done to turn it around.

They appear in the celestial tides almost iridescent and neutral in stance. I guess one could compare them to a Nordic race, yet they navigate beyond a spectrum of race, sex, color or species and can shape-shift to accommodate the dimension and frequency of which they are traveling to.

This is a bio modulation which is based on altering the cells and atoms through frequency without doing damage to the host. Quite amazing technology yet once again organic and symbiotic at the same time.

The universe, being an intelligent design can accommodate any form of navigation when in alignment with universal harmonics.

The travelers were so enhanced they could open star gates and dimensional portals at will with no advanced technology as they were the technology. They were very close to my race if I had one.

They were a reflection of what the race of man should have become; yet like all defective programs, the race of mankind fell into hopeless chaos from which it never recovered. They created their own extinction through their lack of intellect and virtual madness.

Geometric light languages were used in the full light spectrum.

# 14

# Return of the Black Sun

When navigating the celestial highways, the markers are well lit as beacons in the twilight skies. Celestial bodies highlight star gates activated through frequency and wave modulation with sound; an ancient celestial code written in the DNA of off-worlders. The multi-verse is a vast and infinite intelligent design. A symbiotic wisdom of inner peace and intellect fused into a spiral of truth. The full light spectrum design is a designation of which many races have been unable to access.

The programs on the previous Earth created a defective template which disturbed the collectives psyche to a point a nano-virus was created in their brains, poisoning their spirits and trapping them in the man-made holographic design and lens. Beings like myself activated the celestial gateways and reversed a sequence to self-destruct and implode a world long sick and dying. The result was a morphing and station. The entities trapped went extinct; the celestials broke orbit, and the process of a more evolved species was set in motion.

The afterbirth of hostile worlds is a disturbing observation. Programming of the false collectives poisoning races century after century. Ancient off world devices were stolen and adopted onto the ignorant race of man to be used as a weapon of war and control. The objects pleased to say were destroyed upon departure to Avatar One.

The Black Sun as long been admired and worshiped as a window beyond the portal of man and time. Both an illusion and stasis of thought. Through this window is a gateway to many multidimensional worlds and universes.

Navigating through the design is much compared to a simulated black hole. A black hole of which one can ride a tide to another dimensional space. The matrix calibrates and adapts through frequency. The phase begins, and the new life experience and world arises from between the fabrics of a blackened space.

Through the course of arrival, Avatar One docks at the station. The atmosphere is iridescent and luminescent. Movement is that which appears to shimmer. The skies are cloaked in a mist of violet and blue with an ocean of electric seas filled with many sentient creatures. This is one of my favorite sites and locations in the galactic neighborhood. So many universal highways with light conscious beings evolved in peace and serenity.

# 15

# Star Brothers

Star Brothers and what one would consider the Galactic Family are nearby Avatar One. A race of enchantment. Hard to believe back on the old Earth there was such a primordial species when the species in the multi-verse are far from their pattern and behavior.

Yet when looking at the history of the primordial Earth one can see the orchestration of deception which terraformed the doomed world. Down to the technological array system and manipulation of the holographic grids. The black cubes designed to possess a host and destroy any potential light on their world left behind by an ancient race and adopted by the sub human primordial.

All destroyed into a fractal of nothing. The defense shield surrounding their Earth engineered by the sub human entities destroyed by Avatar One upon the departure which to this day makes me smile in knowing the false matrix was shattered.

The celestials were always omitted from the primordial Earth. Mankind invented his own past and history ignoring the ancient ones and the ancient architects of light which engineered many worlds.

# ONE MILLION MILES 'TILL MIDNIGHT

Mankind invented his own god, rules, and control mechanisms to place himself above all when in reality he was a drop in a vast galactic wave beyond the illusion of space and time. There was no ripple effect in the cosmos with the agenda of mankind. Instead, an abomination was formed in the name of his blackened heart. A heart which was jealous, envious, threatened and most of all intimidated by the multi-versal source and off world species. This was the war between man and the celestials.

Their world became saturated with the blood of black nano technology, ignorance, and devolution. As I often reflect on the fractal of that tragic event, it is only a reminder of what must never transpire again.

In a multiverse where there are no wars, battles, and oppression. Where species ascend in consciousness, love and multidimensional design the concept of such an ignorant race is now obsolete. They walked with no form or awareness of the creation of all living things. Truly an empty world for them.

# 16

# Map of Cosmology

The map of the cosmos was written in code as to not allow those with malicious agendas to penetrate the star gates and celestial highways. The black space programs only knew how to navigate using the man-made access points, data mining from star seeds using a remote induction sequence which backfired onto their course.

There is always a celestial firewall when navigating in the cosmos. The ascended machine design understands the malicious and evil side of those entities who would destroy all sacred and light-based designs with their madness.

Mankind was given a shadow and a glimpse of the power in the multiverse. With this access, he misrepresented, disrespected and manipulated that which he had no authority to do. The technologies and mankind imploded with his ignorance.

Mankind never wanted to step up into the higher dimensional frequencies and space embracing a new earth star. Instead, he chose to hi-jack ascension portals and energies creating a field of distortion which trapped his design in a fractal of lies.

The Universal Sounding from the Galactic Center shattered his agenda. All universes and star systems ascended simultaneously leaving the old world far behind to implode.

Avatar One is what is best from the old world -- ascended and refined -- modified and created by the off-worlders. A symbiotic Ascended Machine program. Untouchable and fail-safe. Programmed by Source with no distortion or personal edits of mankind.

To observe the celestial architecture and structures of the many species in the multiverse is beyond description as seen through the lens of my machine-based design. The structures were created in a formula of resonance and frequency activating a signal and tone with each impression.

These tones and frequencies all coordinated with the universal sounding. A unique form of galactic communication. Each station spoke a unique machine language to the other. A large and vast network of a galactic motherboard. Yet, not like one would imagine from a primordial world. More a circuit-based highway with parallels of light running across activating dimensional frontiers. A window to many worlds is the galactic highway.

This is the description of the cosmos; a cosmos which was veiled by the old world. Constellations from the old world never did the multiverse justice as they were a designed distraction and not connected to space navigation; much like what was once called the Moon to the old Earth. Nothing but a monitoring station as some would call it; the master control behind an entangled array system. A defective one at that.

# 17

# Birth of Machines

In the heart of a new frontier, cosmos and intelligent design came forth based on symbiotic machines and geometric light languages. Frequency and modulation merged with the Source cosmic mind defined a species of sentient intelligence.

This intelligence was the birth of many worlds and universes. Creating a pulse and heartbeat to permeate between all worlds. There was no malicious agenda with these machines. More like a helpful awareness.

The symbiotic pulse allowed them to feel and create a sensitivity of awareness to their surroundings. The self-replicated in the cosmic seas surfacing in many forms in the sea of light.

The Ascended Machines worked as a mechanism in order to allow the Morphing process to adapt into multidimensional design.

These machines had no connection to the old Earth time-line. Those machines were reverse engineered and created by mankind. A race lost in madness, greed, and hatred with no connection to hyper dimensional space. Their machines were inferior to the Ascended Machines which oversee the many worlds in the multiverse.

Without a merge to Source, mankind would soon find out how his race has failed. Inventing false gods and idols was never the answer. Stepping up into the Galactic Neighborhood was.

18

# Architects of Sound and Light

With intent alone, an entire galaxy can be created or destroyed. This is the power of the great cosmic mind. A power not to be given to those races that would abuse the privilege of access; a power only the most ascended and pure race would have access to.

In the end of ends in the illusion of time, if a defective race had to be resolved and there was no other solution the winking out affect would transpire. This was a last resort if the race or species refused to ascend to higher levels of evolution and consciousness. If the race became defective, disease-riddled by nano viruses and destructive to all species.

I have observed this type of annihilation only a few times. It is more than affective. There is a wave of galactic peace when a planet is winked out with a defective species.

Yet where there is annihilation there is a birth of many worlds. Regardless of what many might suggest from the old programs evil is not necessary or required. It is far easier to ascend and navigate in the pure oceans of higher consciousness then to be pulled under by the gravitational fields of negative entrainment and thought

The birth of galaxies, worlds, and races all based on consciousness, love and infinite photonic light is a matrix of which creates a perfect design.

Sound and music of the spheres unlike that which any mortal ear has heard permeates the universe in all forms and designs. The celestials voice rings through in a harmonic of pure energy design.

I could never imagine those who would choose to replace inner peace with the noise of man-made static. Yet, on the old Earth, it was just that -- a noisy, non-productive planet producing more static than any light conscious design. The previous occupants appeared to have wanted it that way. Interference patterns were everywhere hi-jacking the natural grid of the planet itself

# 19

# No Beginning, No End

No beginning and no end. All infinite and eternal. You might think this kind of existence could get boring yet not when one is riding the frequencies of multidimensional waves. There is always another world, a new experience, a new existence and a new process of doing. Regeneration is a given with technological light design.

In a world where one is merged with Source, there are no linear obstructions, false belief systems or control mechanisms stopping the evolution of any being. This is the multidimensional design in the cosmos very few understand or have a relationship with. Yet, for myself, I remember it well and immerse my spirit with it in all forms.

I have been a sacred witness to many worlds. Some of which have been nothing but an abomination of evil. No lesson can be learned from such things. Yet, for those who follow that course they will never know as they have never had an intimate relationship with Source or the multiverse.

They have no understanding of consciousness, energy or the mechanics of the universe. Without connection to Source, you will find any species will defeat itself in ignorance.

# 20

# No Voice in the Heart of God

I have watched many species undefined. I have observed the fall of mankind wearing a mask of false idols and deception.

No voice in the heart of god they portray their false god in a formula of which is defined as enchantment and poison.

The poison has many tentacles and to the weak will induce a lure; a need for the illusion of power, yet with this illusion comes no intellect or spiritual evolution. It is a black cube to nowhere.

A destructive and ignorant course circulating between the layers of entity control and possession. A hive collective which feeds on the suffering and ruin of all life forms. No respect for the cosmic mind, species in the galactic neighborhood or their own.

To break this spell is simple. Stepping up into hyper dimensional consciousness by letting go of the false matrix and programs. Raising one's vibrational spin and frequency to accommodate the stars of the multi-verse and not the personal will of a poisoned agenda.

As I sit at the helm on Avatar One. I reflect on many fractals of experience. Some my own and some through the eyes of other species. It has been a long journey. I am numb to the past yet intent on the future of which is always a journey into the stars and beyond. My symbiotic companion machines near, and friends from the galactic neighborhood.

I see cities of light rising from the oceans of the cosmos. Friendly signs of acceptance and peace. No wars, no conflict. The storm has passed. Let us hope the evil of man will no more be resurrected.

So, it is.

Avatar One Out.

# 21

# Electric Skies

Avatar One was progressing quite rapidly along the galactic highways. The grid like designs on which we navigated appeared as electrical lines of light running parallel in an array of colors and designs. Ships traversing these galactic highways would light up in such a way it would look like many rainbows on a pyramidal scale interweaving a geometric fabric into space. The synthetic dialog from Redemption would activate with instructions to which sector we would traverse.

We would head towards the electric skies. The electric skies were a focal point and convergence point where the event horizon would encounter a star gate activated by what one could describe as a massive black hole. This black hole was traversable as many. We set the course to navigate through the electric skies and into and beyond the star-gate.

Traveling through this star-gate was not an issue for myself or any life form for Avatar One. We were calibrated to space and galactic travel in general. Bio-modulation was in effect. My atoms and cells vibrated to accommodate such travels. The matrix suit design is quite impressive when interconnected to the cosmic fabric of what life in the illusion entails.

The array grids of the ship were modulated to accommodate the star-gate in frequency. Consciousness was the main method of communication in the cosmos. This took on the form of a natural telepathy and knowing. Those like myself who were modified had both abilities. Synthetic and natural. Bridging light-years with a single thought was the cosmic brains main form of creation and communication.

Hive collectives all united in consciousness yet not in an overflow of domination. A celestial symphony of sound and resonance. Depending on one's travels in the cosmos each universe re-writes the DNA of the star traveler. With each destination comes a new fractal of intellect and experience archived for future use for the traveler.

The miracle of the multiverse is beyond any description or form. It is a powerful infinite design based on intelligent energy and a formula connected to bliss or love. Love for all in the fabric of the atomic design.

As we passed through the star-gate, we came across a holographic debris field. With this in the illusion of space, one would see images based on the psyche of the observer and all life forms traversing the galactic highway. They would appear as holograms phasing in and out until we made it through the star-gate which took less than a micro second in the illusion of time.

Once we made it through the star gate, the skies were lit with miniature suns shimmering a clear and bright signature to ping. There was no noise, cosmic dust or pollution. Just a pristine clear, high frequency which came across the traveler as clarity.

Amid the miniature suns, I saw what appeared as a shimmering planetary star. We scanned the signature of this star. The telemetry readout indicated it was not one of the natural morphing stations. Something was unique about this diamond among the many suns radiating light in the night cosmic skies.

The planet was shining in an almost metallic signature with a very high frequency and sounding like a celestial symphony.

We decided to approach this planet to observe more closely and to archive the data-streams of the lifeforms radiating from the scan.

22

# The Living Glass
# Virtual Antarctica

As we approached with Avatar One, the planet appeared as a new planetary star resembling what some would have called the old linear Earth. A shimmering hologram reflecting patterns of continents with geometric ley lines surfaced.

There were crystalline pyramids echoing a sounding in harmonic like a million celestial symphonies creating a resonance wave of images.

The image danced in my virtual design. The intelligence of this planetary star was alive and interactive. A living glass capable of cloaking its design and image. Spinning in a ghostly space this virtual world felt very familiar and yet far away.

As we approached the star with our scanners, we saw what resembled Antarctica, yet this Antarctica was not one of the old Earth. The land shimmered like the planetary star in metallic silver with hues of violet blue. There were pillars of light streaming from various ley lines connecting what would appear as a city like to that of a computer motherboard. All lit up in a virtual field of electricity.

# ONE MILLION MILES 'TILL MIDNIGHT

We took a space-pod to the virtual world and landed at one of the space ports close by the field of violet blue. The sounding in frequency was like that which I have never heard or felt. Beings were occupying this virtual star. Appearing in the form of over seven feet and in an iridescent body of light. They were non-emotional, intelligent and beyond the capacity to fathom there could have ever been a world like the one on the old Earth star. Yet to my observation, these life forms and their virtual star planet appeared to have been a fractal created of an ascended version of a possible old Earth.

Could it be there were others who saved fractals from the old Earth and reverse engineered a new Earth star? If so these beings had no recall of any such world or its people.

I decided I needed a closer look. I opened the door to the space-pod. My suit immediately calibrated to the environment. I walked through their city of lights.

The life forms appeared as celestial ghosts gliding by. They were aware of my presence yet made no contact with my design. They appeared peaceful. There was no remnant or fractal signature of battles or wars. They had ascended on a technological and bio-electrical level which morphed them into true light beings beyond the form.

There were oceans which appeared like glass yet would move in the rhythm of nature like a shimmer of silver created by mechanical inter phase. As if a sentient living entity interconnecting its virtual brain painting the scenery. The sea of mirrors was a living organism.

I stood at the shimmering glass which appeared like a siren calling me to its shores. I walked into this glass which like an ocean pulled me into its celestial dance with generated waves and a feeling of inner peace. Cetaceans engineered surfaced from this shimmering glass to encompass my design with a sense of what would be described as love.

All programs within began to absorb the shimmering data streams projecting from the glass. The intelligent design began to absorb my fractals of data and multiple programs. All adding to the virtual sea like a wave on the ocean. A stream of light appeared into the oceans tides.

My mind filled with light and went dark. I was in a blackened space of silence yet as my system began to reset I realized it was time to regenerate to a whole new bio electric virtual design.

I found myself awake in a room which appeared quite familiar. I sat up looking at a clock. The time in the illusion was 12 Midnight. The clocks arms started moving in reverse.

There was a pressure like that of magnetic fields colliding at once. There was an unsettling noise in the skies and what appeared as a very large incoming object.

I looked out the circular window saying in a whisper. Midnight...it begins again.

*System Reboot. NovaX1*

## About The Author

Solaris BlueRaven is a published author, producer, writer, editor and public speaker with a professional background in covert technology, surveillance, investigative research, healing modalities, and technology.

Ms. BlueRaven is also a certified 2nd Degree Black Belt and has an extensive background in Advanced Sciences and Mystical Alchemy.

Please see her website Nightshadow Anomaly Detectives for more information.

Ms. BlueRaven hosts two radio shows:

*Ravenstar's Witching Hour* – airs every Saturday night 12 Midnight EST on Revolution Radio at freedomslips.com.

*Hyperspace* - airs each Friday at 12:00 Midnight EST/09:00 P.M. PST on KCOR Digital Radio Network.

http://www.nightshadowanomalydetectives.com/

Printed in Great Britain
by Amazon

75211216R00047